Georgia's Big Idea

Copyright Notice

Georgia's Big Idea

Written and Illustrated by Dan Byrne

First Printing, 2016

www.littledanes.com

email: contact@littledanes.com

Georgia's Big Idea

Dan Byrne

Georgia the cow lived by the sea,
Munching green grass for her
breakfast and tea.
"Moooo! This is tasty." She often
would say,
"Moooo! This is lovely, I could
eat it all day."

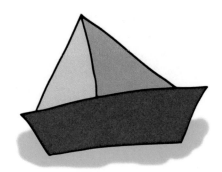

But then one night when the
moon shone so clear,
Georgia woke up with an
enormous idea.
"Oooooh," she thought as she
looked at the sky,
"Oooooh," I'm a cow but I so
want to fly.

To soar like the birds is
                something I'd like
All I need are some wings." So
          she jumped on her bike
"Wings," mooed Georgia as she
                peddled away,
"Wings to fly with I need them
                    today."

So she cycled hard all through
the night,
And arrived at the airport in the
dawn's early light.

"Wings!" said a pilot who was
            checking his plane,
"Wings for a cow! That's really
                        insane.
I've never seen a cow that could
                        fly
Still it might be fun, let's give it
                    a try.

Stand over there while I fetch
you some things,
Stand over there and we'll make
you your wings."
So both of them worked as hard
as they could,
Making new wings from paper
and wood.

" Run," said the pilot, "as hard as
you can.
Run like the wind." So she ran
and she ran.
But poor sad Georgia just
couldn't fly.
Maybe cows weren't meant to
soar into the sky.

"Wheels." Said the pilot, "That's
what you need.
Wheels are the thing that will
give you more speed."
So they tied roller skates, tight
on her feet.
Green little pairs that looked
ever so neat.

"Fly!" Thought the pilot as he
gave her a push,
"Fly like a bird, but don't hit
that bush."
Crash went Georgia head over
heels,
Straight in the bush with a
spinning of wheels.

"Oooohhh! My poor head."
          She mooed out in pain.
"Oooohhh, I'll never go
                    skating again."
"Don't give up" said the pilot,
     "because as tough as it seems,
It's always important to work
               hard for your dreams."
"You're right." Mooed Georgia,
               "I'll never say die.
You're right, it's my dream and
                    I'm going to fly.

There must be a way to soar into
the air,
Maybe balloons tied to a chair.
I could float away up into the
blue,
I could float way admiring the
view."
"No way!" said the pilot, with a
serious frown
"You might go up and never
come down.

You need a plan that's simple
and sound,
You need a plan to get off the
ground.
Now I know a pilot a lady called
Margo,
Who flies a huge plane she fills
full of cargo.
I'm sure if we ask her she'd find
room inside,
I'm sure if we asked her, she'd
give you a ride.

With a parachute on, you could
jump from the plane,
When you've done it once you
can do it again.
Floating away in the sky with the
sun,
Floating away in the sky must be
fun."

So Georgia the cow strapped on
her 'chute,
Along with some goggles and a
skydiving suit.

31

Up soared the plane and Margo
said, "Ready,"
Up soared the plane and Margo
said, "Steady..."
"Here we go," thought Georgia
as she opened the door,
"I'm going to leap like never
before."

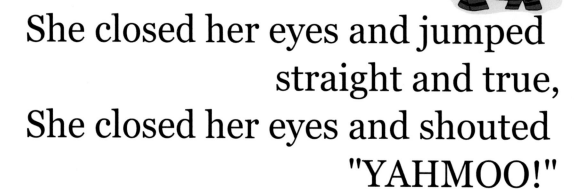

She closed her eyes and jumped
straight and true,
She closed her eyes and shouted
"YAHMOO!"
Whoosh went the parachute
opening wide,
As Georgia started to swoop and
to glide.
"Look at me!" she mooed,
"I'm a cow in the sky.
Look at me." she mooed,
"I'm a cow who can fly!"

75577377R00022

Made in the USA
Middletown, DE
06 June 2018